UFOs: Fact or Fiction?

By

Liam McCann

About the author

Liam McCann was born in Guildford, England, in 1973. He attended Hurstpierpoint College and Staffordshire University, gaining a Bachelor of Arts degree in Sports Physiology and Psychology. Growing up, he excelled on the sports field, becoming county champion in three of the athletics field events and swimming to a national standard. He went on to win a British University medal in 1993. Liam then formed a rock band that toured Europe. The group's highlight came in 2001 when they played to five thousand people. In 2003 he turned his hand to writing non-fiction sports and reference books. He has since had 14 published and is now working on completing his action / thriller series featuring hero Ed Sampson.

He can be contacted via Twitter: @liambmccann
or through his website: www.liambmccann.com

By Liam McCann

When the Messenger meets the King
In the Lap of the Gods
The Devil's Breath
Rolling Thunder
The Battle of Boxhill

Non-fiction

The Olympics Facts, Figures & Fun
Rugby Facts, Figures & Fun
Cricket Facts, Figures & Fun
The Sledger's Handbook
Born to Dribble
The Revised & Expanded Sledger's Handbook
The European Football Championships
UFOs: Fact or Fiction?
Little Book of Survival
Little Book of the Universe
Little Book of Liners
Little Book of HMS Ark Royal

With Sue Todd

Little Book of the Royal Air Force, Red Arrows Edition

With Andrew O'Brien

The World's Greatest Sporting Rivalries

With Hans Potter

The Little English Boy

Introduction

The term unidentified flying object, or UFO, covers a broad range of sightings of mysterious objects in the sky. Because the sightings can't be explained by the observer, many of these events are attributed to alien spacecraft visiting us from other worlds.

In reality, this is unlikely (using our best technology, it would take one of our spaceships 60,000 years just to reach the edge of our solar system), and indeed most sightings can be explained rationally. However, once unusual or secret military aircraft, strange cloud formations, weather balloons, meteorites, satellites, planets, celebratory Chinese lanterns and hoaxes have been ruled out, a small percentage of sightings remain difficult to explain.

Although some of these have been the subject of serious government investigation, it seems likely that, in many cases, military projects were being observed. It's therefore understandable that the government in question doesn't want to probe too deeply into the workings of its own armed forces, and few investigations lead to the publication of credible scientific papers.

But this only rouses the conspiracy theorists who believe our governments are covering up the truth…

Chapter 1 – UFOs throughout history

Many ancient cultures appear to have chronicled UFO visitations in their artwork. Granite carvings dating from 45,000BC in Hunan in Asia, for example, appear to show humans gazing at a series of cylindrical objects hovering in the sky. Rock carvings in Peru from 11,000BC, at Tassili in the Sahara from 6,000BC and from Nambu in Africa from around 4,300BC all depict figures with large, helmet-like heads, and some appear to be wearing spacesuits strikingly similar to those worn by modern astronauts. Early Aboriginal art as well as paintings from a three-thousand-year-old Japanese culture also seem to show spacemen.

Texts from ancient India dating back 5,000 years, and an Egyptian papyrus from 1504BC, describe circles of fire coming from the sky that were brighter than the sun, and there are even references to UFOs in the Bible and ancient Greek and Roman scripts. Many people also believe that the Nazca Lines in Peru (enormous carvings of animals that can only be seen from the air), which date back at least five thousand years, can only have been created by aliens.

Chinese astronomers noticed an unusual object in the night sky 2,500 years ago. They saw it as a religious omen, although today we believe it was probably Halley's Comet. The comet reappears every 76 years or so, so it crops up regularly as a UFO across all cultures and peoples of the world. The Chinese also documented a large 'guest star' in 1054, so called because it could be seen in the sky, night and day, for two years.

We now know this was a result of the supernova explosion that formed the Crab Nebula, which has become the most studied astronomical entity outside our solar system, but Shen Kuo (a government official in the 11th century)'s sighting is not so easily explained.

He recorded similar stories from several eyewitnesses in

Yangzhou, each of whom claimed to have seen a flying object that shone brilliant lights from its open doors before disappearing at extreme speeds. In an age before mechanical technology, this sighting is particularly difficult to explain. Indeed, there were many more cases of unusual objects recorded in the skies during the Middle Ages, an event at Nuremburg in 1561 providing us with several eyewitness accounts. Residents described an hour-long battle between oddly shaped craft that resulted in a crash outside the city. News notices and engravings of the event survive in the Wickiana collection in Zurich.

A bizarre representation of what was apparently seen over Nuremburg in 1561

It was not until 1878 in Denison, Texas, that the words 'flying saucer' entered our language. Farmer John Martin contacted his local newspaper to say that he'd seen a balloon-like object about the size of a saucer flying at 'wonderful speed' (these types of sightings became more common as man took to the air during the First World War).

In 1908 an enormous explosion shook the ground at Tunguska in central Russia, but it took until 1921 before an expedition finally made it to the site. More than 830 square miles of forest had been flattened by the blast but there was no impact crater. Based on a fictional account of the incident by Alexander Kasantsev in 1946, UFO believers claim this was because an enormous extraterrestrial object exploded in the upper atmosphere. It's more likely, however, that a meteorite or comet thirty to fifty metres across blew itself apart five miles above the ground.

In 1917 more than thirty thousand people witnessed the so-called Miracle of the Sun in Fatima, Portugal. Three shepherd children had predicted that the Virgin Mary would appear at noon and many gathered on the hillside to wait for the miracle. After a dull morning, the sun broke through, radiating multicoloured lights and apparently spiralling towards the crowd. Outright panic was avoided but many present believed it signalled the end of the world. Scientists examining the case today cite mass hysteria and hallucinations from prolonged staring at the sun as the most plausible explanation.

During WWII, allied pilots gave the unusual metallic spheres or balls of light that appeared to follow their aircraft a name: foo fighters (in the news today for being Dave Grohl's latest rock band). They were originally thought to be secret German or Japanese weapons but it soon became clear that Axis pilots were reporting similar sightings. Most seemed to be simple fiery spheres like Christmas-tree lights that flew in formation with the aircraft, as if they were under control, before making a few wild turns and vanishing. Despite crews from both sides trying to shoot them down, none was successful. And although the pilots often engaged them, none ever proved to be hostile, leading some people to think that it was only ball lightning, St Elmo's Fire or hallucinations caused by oxygen deprivation.

With all countries in a state of high alert during the war, it is not surprising that there were many false alarms, such as the shelling of a stray weather balloon over Los Angeles in 1942, which almost led to outright panic. After the war, however, sightings often made front-page news. Two incidents in 1947 caught the imagination and caused the UFO phenomena to enter the public consciousness, where it has remained, culturally and psychologically, ever since.

Floating Mystery Ball Is New Nazi Air Weapon

SUPREME HEADQUARTERS, Allied Expeditionary Force, Dec. 13—A new German weapon has made its appearance on the western air front, it was disclosed today.

Airmen of the American Air Force report that they are encountering silver colored spheres in the air over German territory. The spheres are encountered either singly or in clusters. Sometimes they are semi-translucent.

SUPREME HEADQUARTERS, Dec. 13 (Reuter)—The Germans have produced a "secret" weapon in keeping with the Christmas season.

The new device, apparently an air defense weapon, resembles the huge glass balls that adorn Christmas trees.

There was no information available as to what holds them up like stars in the sky, what is in them, or what their purpose is supposed to be.

Businessman Kenneth Arnold was flying his private plane near Mount Rainier in Washington when he apparently saw nine brilliant saucer- and crescent-shaped discs flying across the face of the mountain. His sighting was taken more seriously when an American Airlines crew spotted nine similar objects over Idaho the following week. The national press picked up the incidents, although most tried to explain them as hallucinations or optical illusions. Some, however, believed they might have been secret weapons being tested, or, somewhat predictably, interplanetary visitors.

A few days later, the UFO phenomenon became an international sensation when Walter Haut, an army public information officer, issued a press release saying that personnel from the 509th Bomb Group had recovered parts of a flying saucer from a crash site on a farm in Roswell, New Mexico. Over the intervening years, Roswell has probably become the definitive UFO story. First, there are the sensational headlines. Then comes the official report, which is believed for a time before being questioned by those who have spotted inconsistencies in the story. When the popular conspiracy theories are denied by the military, they are accused of a cover-up and the case can be blown out of proportion.

Chapter 2 – Famous sightings

Roswell, New Mexico

In July 1947 William Brazel noticed some debris – rubber strips, tin foil, paper, scotch tape and toughened sticks – on the Foster farm where he worked. He called Sheriff Wilcox, who then contacted Major Jesse Marcel at the nearby Roswell airbase, and Marcel soon arrived to inspect the site.

Although debris was definitely recovered from the Roswell crash site, and some of it was probably taken to the top secret Hangar 18 at Wright Field (now Wright-Patterson Air Force Base) in Ohio, the Roswell Army Airfield base commander was quick to change Haut's story of the remains coming from a flying disc to them belonging to a high-altitude weather balloon. A press conference was called, the public seemed satisfied and the incident should have been consigned to history.

But physicist and amateur ufologist Stanton Friedman wasn't convinced by the official version of events. In 1978 (no one knows why he waited thirty years) he interviewed Marcel. Marcel claimed that the military had

Debris recovered from the crash site in Roswell hasn't been explained

covered up the crash and recovery of an alien spacecraft. And in 1989 mortician Glenn Dennis claimed that bodies had been found and post mortems had been carried out at the nearby airbase.

Celebrated airman Marion 'Black Mac' Magruder then told his son a strange story about aliens and parts of their spacecraft arriving at Wright Field. He and another man reportedly filmed the autopsies, claiming the four-foot-tall beings had large heads, four spindly digits with no thumbs, no hair and smelled strongly of dead fish. J. Edgar Hoover was so intrigued by what he was hearing that he wrote a memo asking to be allowed access to the disc. When permission was denied, he wrote again to vent his anger at not being given more information.

Senator Barry Goldwater was interviewed about the same incident by Larry King in 1994. He outlined his attempt to be given access to Hangar 18 by Curtis LeMay but the base commander became extremely angry and told the senator never to mention the hangar again.

In response to renewed public interest, the secretary of the air force was ordered to conduct an investigation. In 1995, the first official enquiry appeared to back up the revised version of events because the US was involved in the testing of high-altitude balloons during classified program Mogul, which was using sensitive listening devices to detect Russian nuclear tests.

An artist's impression of project 'Silver Bug'

A second report two years later concluded that the reports of bodies in the area were those of dummies used during high-altitude parachute testing. It is also possible that a secret aircraft codenamed Silver Bug was what had actually crashed and the bodies

15

onboard (chimps were often used in tests) were so badly burned in the resulting fire that those covering the event were confused about what they were seeing. Indeed the Laredo UFO crash near the Texas border in 1948 fits the Silver Bug hypothesis perfectly.

Friedman wasn't so easily swayed though. Having interviewed hundreds of witnesses, he claimed that there was enough evidence to suggest that at least one spaceship had crashed at Roswell and that aliens, some of which may still have been alive, had been recovered. Despite numerous books and films on the subject, opinion is still divided on the most famous UFO case of them all.

Fort Knox, Kentucky

Most of the preceding UFO stories were viewed with a degree of scepticism and were usually taken in good humour, but that attitude changed when Captain Thomas Mantell crashed his aircraft and died while in pursuit of a UFO in January 1948.

The base commander and a number of personnel at Godman Field noticed a large white object with a flaming cone hovering for about an hour near Maysville. Four P-51 Mustangs of the air national guard were already in the air and were ordered to give chase. Three of the pilots turned back when they realised they were low on fuel and didn't have enough oxygen to pursue the object any higher.

Mantell ignored the warnings and climbed to 25,000 feet, where he probably passed out from a lack of oxygen. His aircraft slipped into a long spiral and crashed on farmland in Franklin. Sensational rumours that he was shot down by an alien spacecraft only added to the mystery, although there was no evidence to support this. In fact it seems likely that the UFO was a top secret aluminium skyhook weather balloon, several of which had been launched to the northeast of Fort Knox earlier that day.

A weather balloon is also the likely culprit when analysing George Gorman's account of his dogfight with a UFO in October the same year. Although the pilot claims that the object he engaged showed intelligence and tried to outmanoeuvre his Mustang, his own high speed and quick changes of direction could have contributed to this illusion. Indeed no one on the ground at the Fargo airport control tower in North Dakota reported the UFO making any erratic course changes.

Lubbock, Texas

The town of Lubbock became the centre of the UFO universe in August and September 1951. Three professors from Texas Technical College saw a group of between twenty and thirty lights fly overhead at around 9pm on August 25. As they discussed the unusual sighting a second group flew above the backyard. They reported the incident to the local paper and learned that several other residents had seen a similar event.

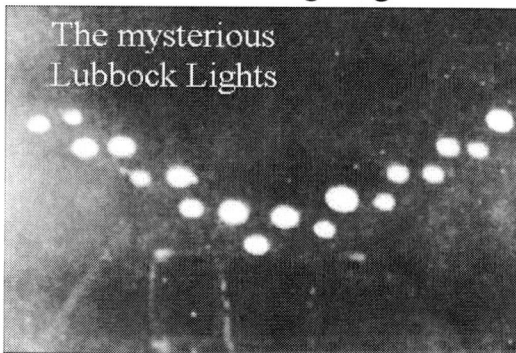
The mysterious Lubbock Lights

Carl Hart, a student at the college, saw a similar flypast the following week. He grabbed his camera in time to photograph two further sightings. The local newspaper published the pictures and the story immediately went nationwide. The images were analysed by Lieutenant Edward Ruppelt from the air force's Project Blue Book (the government agency set up to investigate UFOs) and, although he concluded they weren't a hoax, he couldn't prove they were genuine either. The sighting and the credibility of the eyewitnesses had aroused his interest, however, so he decided to launch a personal investigation.

He concluded that the professors had seen a flock of plovers. Light from new sodium streetlights had reflected from their underbellies and created an unusual illusion. Several local farmers and a number of witnesses agreed as they had seen large numbers of migratory birds that autumn. Although the locals had been as confused as everyone else at first, the birds had then circled some houses and could even be heard squawking.

Not everyone was convinced, however. No one could replicate the Hart photos and the objects were said to be far too large to be birds. Given that he had championed the plover explanation, it came as something of a surprise when Ruppelt made an abrupt U-turn in his 1956 book on the subject. Confusingly, however, having rejected the bird theory, he failed to say what was really responsible for the sightings.

Some believed that the lights were coming from the air force's new flying wing, but, as no one could explain the lack of jet noise, the incident has become another of the more unusual and inexplicable UFO cases.

Lancaster, New Hampshire

The first and perhaps most important case of abduction by aliens apparently happened to Betty and Barney Hill while they were driving home to Portsmouth in September 1961. When a strange light appeared and gradually drew closer, they stopped the car for a better look and so they could walk their dog. As they continued their journey along Route 3, the brightly lit object continued following them.

A couple of miles further on, the object descended rapidly and forced them to stop. Barney grabbed his binoculars and a pistol and jumped out. He claimed to have seen around ten non-human figures, one of which communicated with him telepathically, asking him to stay where he was and keeping looking straight ahead. Barney panicked and returned to the car and the couple drove off at high speed.

A short time later they heard odd noises from the car and their senses dulled. When they eventually arrived home they still felt strange and couldn't explain their broken watches and several marks on the vehicle. As they couldn't remember what had happened, the following morning they telephoned Pease Air Force Base to report the encounter. Without being given most of the detail, Major Paul Henderson concluded that they had probably seen an optical illusion involving the planet Jupiter.

Ten days after the event Betty began having vivid dreams about their abduction and examination by the humanoid figures. Because neither of the Hills could remember anything from the last 35 miles of their journey, they began to suspect something more sinister had happened and they eventually agreed to undergo regression hypnosis.

Doctor Benjamin Simon tested the couple over a six-month period in 1964. Their stories agreed on a number of points and both became extremely anxious and upset during the sessions. However, Simon concluded that the event was entirely inspired by Betty's unusual dreams, which had themselves probably been influenced by a crop of recent science-fiction films – such as 1953's *Invaders from Mars* – although he accepted this couldn't explain every aspect of the supposed encounter.

And there things should have stayed were it not for reporter John Lutrell being given tapes of a lecture the Hills had give on the subject in 1963. They were suddenly front-page news across the nation and everyone's attention was attracted to a star map drawn by Betty. When analysed, it appeared to show the aliens coming from the Zeta Reticuli double-star system, although most serious cosmologists have dismissed it as a random drawing.

We may never know what really happened that night, but the incident made celebrities out of the Hills and spawned a number of books and films, most notably *The Interrupted Journey* and *The UFO Incident*.

Berwyn Mountain, Wales

In January 1974 an incident in the mountains of North Wales became known as Roswelsh. Several unusual lights were seen in the sky before the ground started shaking. Two explanations were given by locals who searched the area but found nothing: either a meteorite had exploded in mid-air or a UFO had crashed.

A plausible scientific explanation has been given, however. Although people were sceptical at the time, a phenomenon known as earthquake lights could have been responsible. When the earth's crust comes under strain before seismic activity, strange lights, thought to be electromagnetic, often appear in the sky above the fault. These lights were first photographed during the Nagano earthquake swarm in Japan in the mid-1960s and have since been observed prior to many 'quakes worldwide, including the massive Indian Ocean tsunami in 2004.

The British Geological Survey concluded that a magnitude 3.5 earthquake had struck North Wales that night, but there was no explanation given for the ufologists' claims that non-human bodies had been recovered by police and that local residents has been visited by 'men in black'.

Colares, Brazil

During the last three months of 1977 the Brazilian island of Colares apparently came under attack from mysterious beams of radiation that left puncture wounds and burn marks on more than thirty victims. The government was suitably concerned and dispatched a team (codenamed Saucer) to investigate. Their report was classified for nearly twenty years.

Dr Wellaide Cecim Carvalho, a local resident and witness, examined several of the victims and concluded that

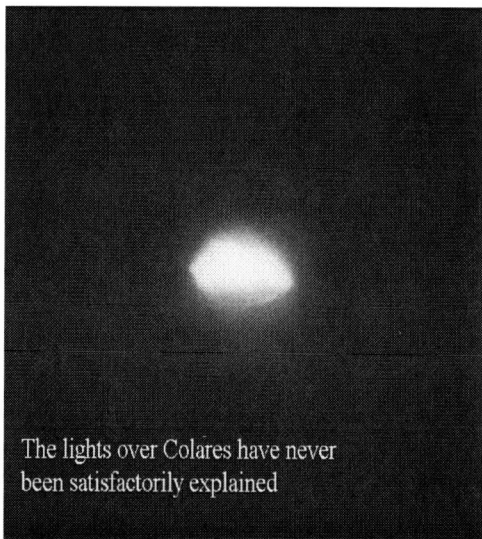

The lights over Colares have never been satisfactorily explained

they were suffering from severe headaches, low blood pressure and anaemia. Most had burn marks and permanent hair loss where they'd been struck by the light beams and two later died of their injuries. She was also targeted by the lights but avoided illness or injury.

In 2004 more documents from Operation Saucer were finally released by the Brazilian air force. Some claimed that the investigative team had witnessed the lights themselves and had even taken photographs of luminous, umbrella-shaped spheres emitting powerful beams of radiation. Brazilian authorities, including the air force, have repeatedly stated that they have no explanation for the event.

Rendlesham Forest, Suffolk, England

In the forest surrounding RAF Woodbridge, tens of USAF personnel saw unexplained lights and a craft apparently landing over the Christmas period in 1980. A number of servicemen entered the forest thinking that an aircraft had crashed but they soon saw strange lights moving through the trees and heard nearby farm animals in a state of panic. Sergeant Jim Penniston later claimed to have touched the craft and made detailed notes about its appearance, but his story has changed many times over the years and is usually discredited.

The police found nothing in the forest when they arrived in the early hours of the morning. They concluded that supposed landing marks were rabbit warrens, the animals were probably startled Muntjac deer, and the lights were from a landing beacon at nearby RAF Bentwaters and also from Orford Ness Lighthouse a few miles away. Indeed, on a live recording made by deputy base commander Lieutenant Charles Halt two nights later, one airman can be heard calling out as the strange lights reappear. The timing coincides with the frequency of the lighthouse's sweep. Other explanations for the lights on the first night include the widely reported re-entry of a Soviet satellite.

Despite the police version, Halt remains adamant that they witnessed an extraterrestrial visit and that the event was covered up by the US and UK. Because the incident occurred near a nuclear base, the Ministry of Defence immediately put together a file on the subject and it was quickly labelled Britain's Roswell.

Glons, Belgium

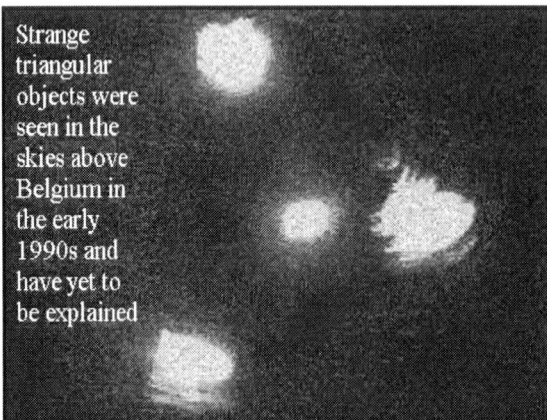

Strange triangular objects were seen in the skies above Belgium in the early 1990s and have yet to be explained

The Belgian UFO wave, as it became known, lasted from November 1989 until April 1990, peaking on the night of March 30. During this five-month period, an estimated fourteen thousand people saw unidentifiable objects in the sky, two-and-a-half-thousand of whom submitted witness statements describing the event.

Two F-16 fighters were scrambled from Beauvechain Airbase after hundreds of witnesses reported seeing brightly lit triangular-shaped craft performing erratic manoeuvres in the night sky on March 30. The targets were tracked by radar but the fighters were unable to intercept them and they repeatedly climbed to 10,000 feet, accelerating from 140mph to 1,100mph before descending to ground level in just five seconds. Peak *g*-forces during these manoeuvres would have been fatal for human pilots.

Although experts suspect that helicopters were responsible for some of the radar contacts, the incident as a whole has never been properly explained.

Space

The crews of both Gemini VII and XI reported seeing strange objects during their orbital spaceflights but, despite a few minutes of audio recording and a couple of inconclusive photos taken by the astronauts, no video data exists. The Apollo crews also reported a number of strange sightings, but these can usually be explained as orbital debris from their booster rockets.

During the 29th shuttle mission in March 1989, crewman John Blaha aboard *Discovery* can be heard to say: "Houston, this is *Discovery*, we still have the alien spacecraft under observance." NASA initially refused to confirm whether the recording was genuine but, when repeatedly questioned about it, said that it was probably a joke on Blaha's part.

In 1991 the crew of the same shuttle videoed flashes of light and several objects that seemed to be flying in a controlled fashion. When NASA technicians examined the footage they concluded the objects were simply ice particles and the flashes of light came from the shuttle's own thrusters. Despite a number of scientists disagreeing with this official version, ice particles have been known to decelerate in a uniform manner in the upper atmosphere, and there are countless small items of debris and orbiting junk from satellites and old rocket stages that burn up as their orbits gradually deteriorate.

The shuttle *Columbia* recorded hundreds of objects on a specialised camera that could see in the non-visible spectrum in 1996 and the same orbiter picked up unusual images during another mission later in the year. All were eventually explained as orbital debris reflecting in sunlight. The crew of *Discovery* filmed yet more unusual goings on over Washington in 2001 during STS-102, but this time the objects appeared to start, stop and accelerate as if under intelligent control and the incident has yet to be explained.

Phoenix, Arizona

Late one evening in March 1997, a series of lights and UFOs were seen across Arizona and Nevada by thousands of people. The USAF admitted to having aircraft in the area and claimed the lights were simply flares being dropped during a training mission. Video footage from a number of eyewitnesses disputes this official version, however. The lights do not fall and fade as if they are flares, and several hundred people report seeing an enormous triangular or V-shaped craft travelling silently (or with the faint sound of rushing wind) through the hills above the city.

The sighting has now been categorised into two separate events, the first of which was the wedge-shaped object that slowly travelled south across the entire state of Arizona. Despite a number of theories, no satisfactory explanation has been given for this sighting. The second event revolves around nine lights seen above Phoenix from around 10pm. The military stands by its explanation that they were long-burning slow-falling flares, but Arizona Governor Fife Symington, a key witness and expert pilot, claims that: "It couldn't have been flares because it had the definite outline of a geometric shape, and flares don't fly in formation."

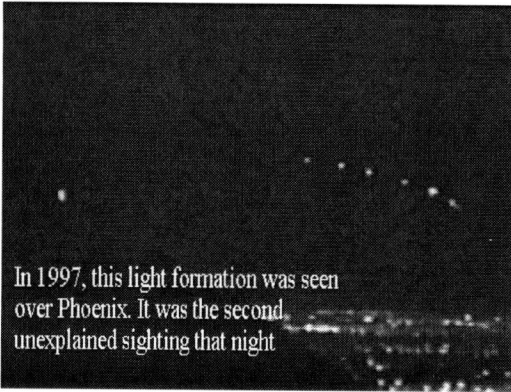
In 1997, this light formation was seen over Phoenix. It was the second unexplained sighting that night

Similar events involving large triangular craft hovering before moving away at high speed were reported by various witnesses, including five policemen in the early hours of January 5, 2000 in southern Illinois, and over Chicago's O'Hare airport a few years later. More recently, video footage has emerged from South Wales showing lights appearing to move in formation, and a police helicopter supposedly took evasive action before giving chase to a brightly lit UFO near Cardiff in 2008.

The Phoenix incident, however, remains one of the most perplexing cases, primarily because it was witnessed by so many people. A version of events even made it into the plot of a horror film, 2007's *Night Skies* starring Jason Connery.

Stephenville, Texas

In January 2008, hundreds of residents in the small town of Stephenville reported seeing F-16 fighters chasing UFOs ranging in size from small triangular craft to enormous discs up to a mile long. The US air force initially denied there were any jets in the area but later conceded that it was conducting training flights. Radar data obtained from the federal aviation authority confirmed that ten F-16s and one unidentified object were picked up in the area reported by the witnesses.

When pressed for more detail about the UFO, the air force has declined to comment, but many of the witnesses believe they probably saw a top-secret reconnaissance aircraft, the stealth drone RQ170 Sentinel, the existence of which was denied until December 2009. Other people claim the larger craft was probably a stealth blimp, a silent and undetectable high-altitude surveillance balloon. This has also been given as an explanation for the mysterious craft seen over Phoenix in 1997.

Chapter 3 – The conspiracy theories

As curious humans, we love a good conspiracy theory. Most of them can be debunked quite quickly because no one ever admits to being part of the conspiracy. Take the Apollo moon landings. A large number of people across the globe don't believe we had the technology to go to the moon, and, even if we did, the astronauts couldn't have survived the large doses of stellar radiation. Also, shadows in the crystal clear photos diverge so there must have been two light sources; there's no blast crater under the lander; the flag appears to wave when there should be no atmosphere; the list of apparent anomalies goes on and on.

All of these issues are easily explained: the astronauts were only exposed to the radiation for short periods of time; where two shadows hit different gradients they often diverge; NASA only released the best photos – thousands have never been seen by the public – the low gravity on the moon and small power output of the lander wouldn't leave a crater, and the flag only moves when touched etc.

Some us want to believe that Princess Diana's death wasn't an accident, or that Lee Harvey Oswald couldn't have acted alone when assassinating President Kennedy, or that the US government was somehow behind the attacks on 9/11. We like to look for patterns and meaning where there are none, order where there is chaos.

The simplest explanation for events is usually the best, however. No government in the world has ever plugged all of its leaks, so is it really plausible that hundreds of lighting technicians, film cameramen, base staff, radar operators around the world who tracked the spacecraft, thousands of NASA employees and the astronauts themselves could have remained silent for more than forty years about the missions to the moon?

No one with any credibility has ever stepped forward to

say they were part of a deception on a massive soundstage at a secret location. If you don't accept the missions as fact, you simply have to check the pictures taken by the Lunar Reconnaissance Orbiter (which clearly show the landing sites), or, if you're still not convinced, the data collected at the McDonald Observatory in Texas (one of many sites) from laser retro-reflectors on the moon's surface details exactly how far the moon is from Earth based on the time it takes the laser to reflect back to the receiver. This data proves that someone must have placed the reflectors on the moon. The conspiracy theorists, incidentally, have no explanation for this and usually avoid the subject.

We don't want to accept that Princess Diana died in a car crash because, despite Occam's Razor (when you stick to the known facts, the simplest explanation is usually the best), it's *too* simple. There must be more to the story than a drunk driver colliding with another car and then losing control. (Several reputable sources believe the police eventually found the driver of the infamous white Fiat Uno but have spared the driver a lifetime in the media spotlight by refusing to name them.)

So, why couldn't Oswald have shot Kennedy? He was a competent marksman who was sympathetic to the Cuban cause and had a grudge against the president, he ordered the rifle, worked in the book depository and his fingerprints were on the weapon when it was found. Surely there must be more to it than that. There is, but it only implicates Oswald further. His death at the hands of Jack Ruby in full view of the nation a couple of days later was what kick-started the conspiracy theories. If he'd confessed or made it to trial and had been convicted, much of the furore that has since transpired would never have happened.

The terrorist attacks on 9/11 are a little different because the US government and its military were caught cold by a ruthless and determined enemy. Because it took so long for them to react, and mistakes were made during the investigation (understandable when the complexity and scale of the task is considered), conspiracy theorists are quick to pounce, but the cover-ups and incompetence occurred *after* the attacks had taken place, not before. It is inconceivable that a government would knowingly kill thousands of its own people without someone blowing the whistle, yet no one has ever admitted to being part of a conspiracy.

However, because some credible witnesses have come forward regarding the recovering of crashed UFOs and the filming of aliens, the extraterrestrial conspiracy might hold water:

Area 51

The military base at Groom Lake in Nevada is one of the most secret installations in the world (the US government refused to acknowledge it existed until 2003). For this reason, it has become the subject of countless conspiracy theories, from being the film set where the moon landings were faked to the place where the spacecraft that crashed at Roswell is now kept. Even the main road leading to Groom Lake Road is known as the Extraterrestrial Highway.

During the Second World War, Groom Lake was used for artillery and bombing exercises before being abandoned until 1955. It was then taken over by Lockheed during the trials of the U-2 spy plane (by 1957, 50% of all UFO sightings were attributed to the U-2). They expanded the base and built the first runway but the U-2 development program was interrupted by a number of nuclear tests. The U-2's successor (OXCART) eventually became the SR-71 Blackbird, and all the variants in between were also tested at Groom Lake, as were the prototype Stealth Fighters, the F117 Nighthawks. During the 1980s and early 19990s the base was further expanded while access to the surrounding mountains became prohibited.

The area's secrecy and mythical status have been enhanced by signs threatening lethal force should anyone breach the base perimeter. Even military pilots are likely to face disciplinary action if they stray into restricted airspace, and astronauts have been instructed not to point their cameras at the site. The outskirts of the base are patrolled by armed security teams in SUVs, while video surveillance cameras and motion sensors alert them to any intruders. There have been no violent confrontations reported, although heavy fines and follow-up visits from government

An aerial view of the top-secret facility at Groom Lake that is known as Area 51

officials have been documented.

This over-the-top security has prompted many people to speculate that Area 51 has much to hide from the outside world. Some believe that programmes to reverse engineer

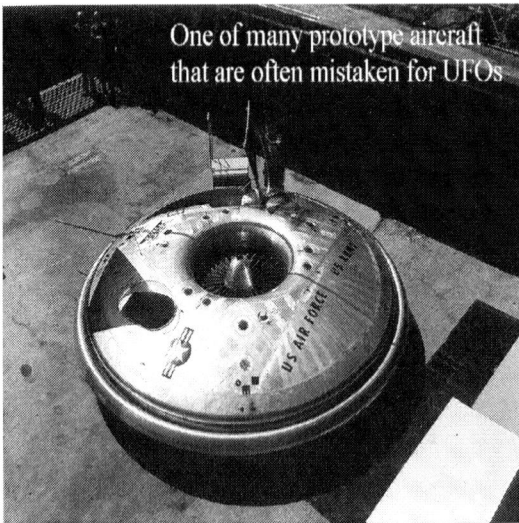

One of many prototype aircraft that are often mistaken for UFOs

the Roswell spaceship have already proved successful, and that the surviving alien(s) have been willing assistants (to most people it seems inconceivable that humans could progress from using the horse and cart to walking on the moon within eighty years unless alien technology was used to develop new programmes). They also believe that exotic propulsion

30

systems, time-travel technology and top-secret weapons are also being developed at the base.

The latter arguments are almost certainly true. Groom Lake has been used to design and manufacture all kinds of experimental aircraft for more than half a century, several of which have been mistaken for UFOs by keen observers and passing pilots. And the supersonic combustion ramjets allegedly used during the hypersonic Aurora's development will probably have been tested there. Time travel is one of the aims of modern science and it's no secret that governments the world over are working on such projects.

Where the situation becomes a little murky, however, is on the subject of crashed alien craft and their occupants. In 1989 Bob Lazar claimed to have worked on an alien spaceship at the Papoose Lake site of Area 51. He mentioned examining nine different discs, which he originally believed to be of terrestrial origin. When he studied their propulsion systems, however, he changed his mind and concluded they couldn't have been manufactured on Earth. He was then briefed about the 100,000-year-long relationship between humans and aliens from the Zeta Reticuli star system 39 light-years from Earth.

If this all sounds a little far-fetched, it's worth looking into Lazar's background. He claimed to have studied physics and gained degrees from both the California and Massachusetts Institutes of Technology but no record of him can be found there (he says the government is erasing his personal details). UFO investigator Stanton Friedman and Dr David Morgan looked at his theory regarding the supposed propulsion systems and concluded that he barely understood current physical laws and his scientific credentials were both troubling and puzzling. He also references the Zeta Reticulans, the alien beings that cropped up during the famous Hill abduction case.

In 2004 Dan Crain announced that he had worked at Area 51 with an extraterrestrial being known as J-Rod (a telepathic translator) on cloning alien viruses. He also said he met angels in his lab and they conversed in Hebrew. Again, it seems that credibility is the biggest obstacle to being taken seriously. Crain claimed to have earned his doctorate from Stony Brook University in New York when he actually got a BA in psychology from the University of Nevada. He was apparently working as a parole officer and volunteer teacher at a kids' club rather than as a government operative at Area 51.

Now that Area 51 has become widely known, it has been reported that the US military is scouting for alternate locations from where to conduct its secret 'Black' projects. One such site is supposedly at Green River in Utah, although the base that did exist here in the 1960s has fallen into disrepair.

AUTEC

The secretive Atlantic Undersea Testing and Evaluation Centre on Andros Island in the Bahamas 180 miles southeast

The navy equivalent of Area 51 is on Andros Island in the Bahamas

of West Palm Beach in Florida is the naval equivalent of Area 51. It was built on the edge of an ocean basin around a hundred miles long and over a mile deep in the mid-'60s to provide the US and UK with a base for establishing and maintaining naval superiority over the Russians during the Cold War. Boasting acoustic and weapons testing ranges, the site's sophisticated technology can track, monitor and target a variety of airborne, surface and sub-surface vessels.

It seems likely that a large number of mysterious sightings in this part of the Bermuda Triangle can be explained by secretive military tests of submersibles and exotic aircraft, but that doesn't stop the conspiracy theorists claming visitors from other worlds must be behind the strange lights and radar targets that occasionally appear in the waters and the sky around Andros Island. And the military test hypothesis can't explain why Christopher Columbus monitored a glimmering light that danced up and down during the night on his voyage past the islands to the New World in 1492.

Chapter 4 – Famous hoaxes

The Aurora UFO incident, Texas

In 1897 the small town of Aurora had experienced a run of bad luck – the cotton crop had failed, a fire had killed several residents and a spotted fever epidemic had claimed more lives – and the news that the planned railroad was no longer coming through town was the last straw for local man S. Haydon, so he decided to put the place back on the map with an elaborate UFO hoax.

He capitalized on the fact that a mysterious cigar-shaped airship had been seen across the United States during the previous year (there were at least three sightings, all of which have been debunked as hoaxes) and claimed that such a craft had collided with a windmill on Judge Proctor's land in early April. The pilot, a strange Martian being, didn't survive the impact and was buried in the local cemetery.

Today, the believers and non-believers are still divided on whether this really was an elaborate hoax or if something did crash in the town. KDFW TV found clues supporting a crash but that there was nothing to suggest the craft was of extraterrestrial origin. The Mutual UFO Network (MUFON) found a rare aluminium alloy and a grave marked with a saucer-shaped object. A *UFO Hunters* investigation used ground-penetrating radar to examine the site but the grave had deteriorated and their results were inconclusive.

Aztec, New Mexico

Since the Roswell incident the previous year there had been a fair amount of interest in the UFO phenomenon. So when oil workers apparently stumbled on a downed alien spacecraft in 1948, the media geared up for another sensational story. The oilmen contacted writer Frank Scully (after whom the *X-files* character is named) and told him that they thought the high-powered radar favoured by the military had apparently interfered with the craft's systems and brought the large flattish disc down.

Scully promptly wrote a book about the event called *Behind the Flying Saucers*, in which sources close to the oilmen, Silas Newton and Dr Gee, claimed that the disc was nearly a hundred feet across and contained the bodies of several dead alien beings.

Despite reporter J. Cahn exposing the episode as a hoax a couple of years later (the oilmen had counted on a gullible Scully believing their story and committing it to print – the book sold 60,000 copies), an FBI memo discovered in 1960 appeared to corroborate Scully's story. It said that at least three crash sites had been investigated, and further examination of the case by Canadian radio engineer Wilbert Smith revealed that details in the book were accurate, the saucers were not of this Earth and the whole thing was classified higher than the hydrogen bomb. It seems more likely, however, that Newton and the mysterious Dr Gee (probably Leo GeBauer) had fed the FBI false statements.

Crop circles, Wiltshire

In the 1970s several unusual formations appeared overnight in the fields of southern England. When they saw the way the crops had been flattened, ufologists immediately became interested in the phenomenon because they believed some of the shapes were too complex to have been created by humans.

Paranormal investigators studied the formations for years but couldn't replicate the more exotic circles, so they were eventually attributed to UFOs or strange downdrafts caused by the ionisation of the air. In 1991, however, Doug Bower and Dave Chorley finally admitted to making several circles with nothing more than a few lengths of rope and a pair of wooden planks.

Their secret out, more impressive circles began to appear. Despite fiercely defending their belief that the circles are not made by humans, supporters of the cause, indeed the study of UFOs in general, have been labelled, some would say harshly, under the pseudoscience heading.

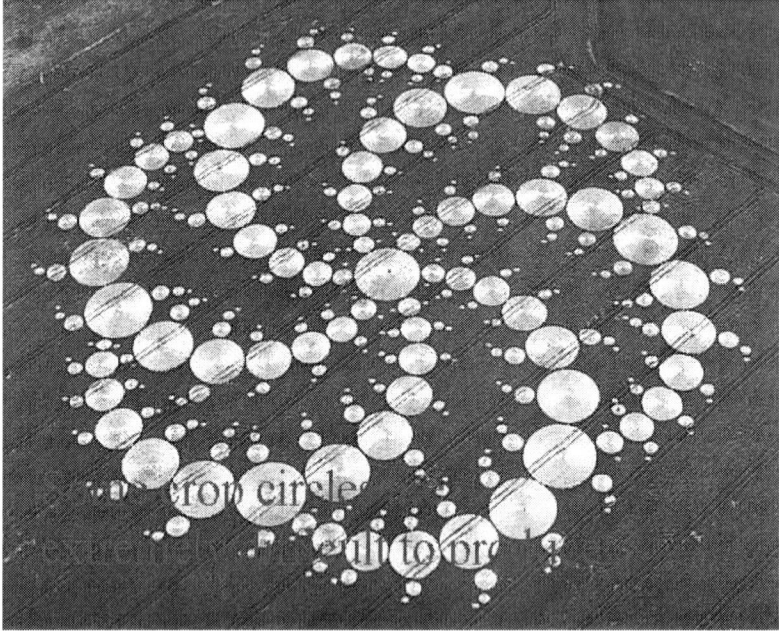

When an especially complex circle appears, the ufologists are quick to say it couldn't have been made by people. Sadly for them, the hoaxers then usually step forward with evidence documenting how they did it.

Alien autopsy

In 1992, entrepreneur Ray Santilli claimed to have been given a film showing the autopsy of an alien recovered from the Roswell crash site. The poor-quality seventeen-minute black-and-white film caused a media sensation around the world when it was shown in forty countries in 1995. However, many of those interviewed for the accompanying documentary already believed it was a hoax, but the television stations insisted their comments were not broadcast for fear of harming the ratings.

After the film had aired, director John Jopson, along with many others associated with the documentary, immediately declared that he thought the footage was nonsense.

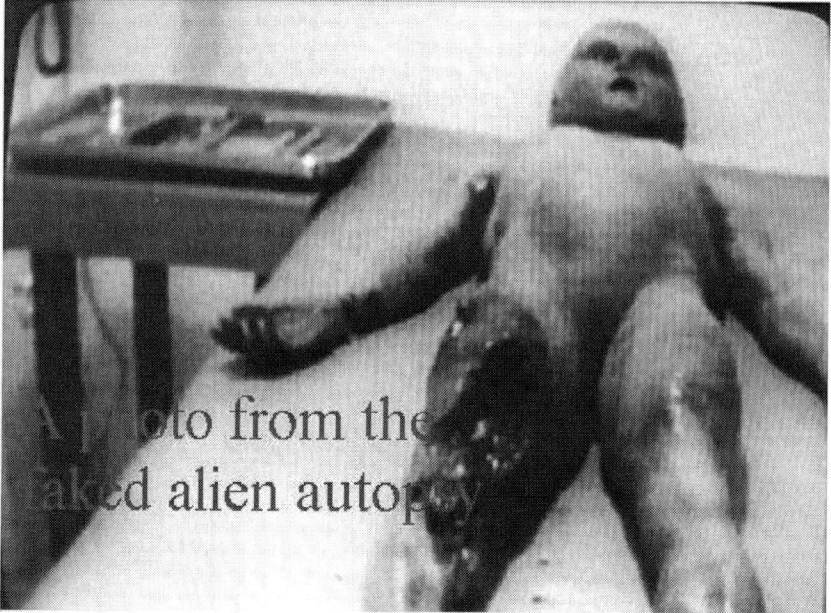

A photo from the faked alien autopsy

Santilli was forced to concede that most of the original footage was of such poor quality that he'd insisted the scene be re-shot as a reconstruction of actual events, with a few of the original frames still making the final cut, although he never said which parts were genuine.

It was eventually revealed that artist and sculptor John Humphreys had made two alien bodies, which had then been filled with sheep's brains surrounded in jam, chicken entrails and knuckle joints sourced from a local butcher. Santilli maintains that the film is an accurate reconstruction of the original but degraded footage.

Turkey

Yalcin Yalman, night guard at the Yeni Kent compound in

Turkey, filmed several hours of footage of enormous UFOs in the summer of 2008. The chairman of the Sirius Space Science Research Centre concluded that the footage was genuine and labelled the images the most important UFO pictures ever. The images could not be attributed to manmade objects such as aircraft or helicopters, and he also ruled out planets and meteorites and any sort of meteorological explanation. Although the footage remains inconclusive to some experts, many people now believe it to be an elaborate computer-generated hoax. Why, after all, did Yalman carry on filming night after night for four months when the first few images would have caused an international sensation?

Morristown, New Jersey

On the evening of January 5 2009, residents of Morris County reported seeing five strange lights in the sky. Control tower personnel also saw the lights but couldn't work out what they were coming from because nothing appeared on their radar. The sightings continued across the county throughout January and February, spooking some locals into believing they were being visited by extraterrestrials. The remaining theories revolved around supernatural phenomena, helicopters with cargo, surveillance blimps, secret military projects and an elaborate hoax.

On April 1, Joe Rudy and Chris Russo admitted that they had been behind the stunt. They simply attached lights to helium balloons and released them near Morristown to demonstrate how easy it was to design a hoax to fool UFO experts. Their results proved how widely people's stories varied, with some saying they'd never seen anything so scary, others claiming there was no way they could be balloons, and still more saying how fast they were moving in all different directions. Dorian Vicente even went as far as saying that nine scattered lights eventually aligned, and Ray

Vargas thought they must be communicating with each other.

British scientists conducted an experiment to prove how susceptible people become when a seemingly ordinary situation is misinterpreted. They weighted a stick so that it would bob up and down out of the water and dropped it into a lake at a university in Scotland. Almost everyone they asked said it was a stick or submerged log but, when they repeated the experiment in Loch Ness, almost everyone thought it was the mythical monster and some people claimed to have seen its head quite clearly.

Chapter 5 – UFOs in popular culture

There have been many fictional portrayals of Area 51 and the UFOs it supposedly houses in books, music and film. Extraterrestrials, time travel and sinister conspiracies, such as the Roswell incident, tend to feature heavily. At the end of *Raiders of the lost Ark*, for example, the artefact is buried in Hangar 51, and the same hangar makes a brief reappearance in the alien-influenced sequel *Indiana Jones and the Kingdom of the Crystal Skull*, where it has been used to store one of the alien corpses from the Roswell incident. The television series *Seven Days* is based at Area 51, and numerous video games have also included Groom Lake.

The most notable film, TV and musical references to the UFO culture are listed below:

The War of the Worlds

The 1898 sci-fi novel by H.G. Wells was one of the first to chronicle the conflict between earthlings and an alien race as the hero tries to survive an unprovoked Martian attack. As the invaders devastate much of southern England, the book's narrator desperately searches for his wife. Just when it seems the capital of the British Empire will fall to the rampant Martians, they succumb

A drawing by Brazilian artist Henrique Alvim Corrêa showing a Martian machine battling with the warship HMS Thunder Child

to terrestrial bacteria, against which they have no immunity. The book is still in print today and remains widely read and referenced.

A radio broadcast of the story, which had been adapted to make it sound like a newscast, was aired by actor and filmmaker Orson Welles in 1938. It caused a sensation because millions of people, already uneasy about the prospect of war with Germany, believed the invasion to be true, although claims that there was outright panic across America are probably exaggerated.

The book and radio play have spawned numerous film and TV spin-offs – including the blockbuster of the same name starring Tom Cruise in 2005 – and undoubtedly influenced the writing of authors like Arthur C. Clarke and Michael Crichton. Jeff Wayne's progressive rock musical interpretation of the story starring Richard Burton, David Essex and Phil Lynott was released in 1978. The album reached number one in eleven countries and is listed as the fortieth best-selling work of all time in the UK. The episode even got a mention in the Queen song *Radio Ga Ga*.

The Day the Earth Stood Still

FROM OUT OF SPACE....
A WARNING AND AN ULTIMATUM!

THE DAY THE EARTH STOOD STILL

MICHAEL RENNIE · PATRICIA NEAL · HUGH MARLOWE

This 1951 film capitalised on the huge interest around the alleged UFO crashes in New Mexico. Indeed the vast majority of Hollywood sci-fi films from the 1950s and '60s used Martians arriving in flying saucers as their main theme. At a time when the US and Soviet Union were 'fighting' the Cold War and engaged in the space race, moviemakers realised they had almost guaranteed success with films of the genre. The story, which sees a human-like alien

41

come to Earth to warn people about how the errors of their ways will lead to the destruction of the plant, was remade as a big-budget blockbuster starring Keanu Reeves in 2008.

Invasion of the Body Snatchers (1956)

The four films based on Jack Finney's novel – it was remade in 1978, 1993 and 2007 – follow the same basic plot. The resident human population on Earth begins to notice that their friends and family seem to have had their personalities altered. When people fall asleep, alien seed pods that have been drifting through space make exact duplicates of them. The pod people are indistinguishable from those they are replacing apart from showing a complete lack of emotion. The epidemic spreads as people who are desperately trying to stay awake eventually fall asleep and are replaced.

There is no doubt that films like this and *Invaders from Mars* influenced the crop of contemporary television series that appeared in the 1960s. *Doctor Who* (1963), *Lost in Space* (1965) and the animated comedy classic, *The Jetsons*, which originally ran in 1962-63 before reappearing twenty years later, were among the most popular and continue to be referenced today. The genre even spawned a number of music acts, with Britain's hard rocking UFO (formed in 1969) perhaps the most influential.

Close Encounters of the Third Kind (1977)

This seminal film follows Roy Neary (Richard Dreyfuss)

after he experiences a close encounter with a UFO. He becomes increasingly obsessed with the phenomenon after locals are reportedly kidnapped by the aliens. Although UFO activity gradually increases around the world, it eventually becomes clear that their intentions are not hostile, a theme continued with another Stephen Spielberg epic, *E.T. the Extra-Terrestrial*, in 1982.

For many, *E.T.* remains the greatest science-fiction film of all time. It revolves around the friendship a lonely boy, Elliott (Henry Thomas), has with an extraterrestrial being stranded on Earth, and their efforts to return the alien to its rightful home.

Independence Day

In director Roland Emmerich's 1996 big-budget blockbuster, alien spacecraft spread out above the world's major cities on July 2. It soon becomes apparent that they're planning to attack. Retaliatory strikes by US and other forces fail and survivors are eventually corralled at Area 51.

Captain Stephen Hiller (Will Smith) and computer expert David Levinson (Jeff Goldblum) then use an alien spaceship recovered at Roswell to launch a counter-attack against the invading fleet. They

upload a virus into the mother-ship to disable the shields of the drones before planting a nuclear bomb to destroy it.

43

The film capitalised on moviegoers' demand for epic disaster films in the mid-1990s and grossed over eight hundred million dollars worldwide, then the second highest box office take. It won an Oscar for best visual effects.

In June 2011, Emmerich and producer Dean Devlin announced that they had come up with plots for two sequels. It is interesting to note that the number of UFO sightings across the world jumped markedly in the months after the original film's release, so it's likely we can expect another wave of sightings in 2013.

Mars Attacks! and *Men in Black*

Dating from the mid-1990s, these two films offer a more humorous take on the alien phenomenon. Boasting an all-star cast (Jack Nicholson, Glenn Close, Pierce Brosnan, Sarah Jessica Parker, Danny DeVito), *Mars Attacks!* kept its tongue firmly in its cheek and took a black comedic and satirical swipe at numerous B-movies.

A CGI Martian from Mars Attacks!

Although the Martians are hell bent on taking over the world, it is eventually discovered that they can be killed by subjecting them to the Slim Whitman song *Indian Love Call*.

Starring Will Smith and Tommy Lee Jones, *Men in Black* (and its equally entertaining sequels) suggests that aliens have always lived among us. They are monitored by a top-secret intelligence agency, MIB, which soon discovers alien activity is increasing. A 'bug' has been sent to Earth to recover a miniature galaxy hidden somewhere in New York. When the guardian of the galaxy is killed, his government tries to destroy the Earth rather than letting the galaxy fall into the bug's hands. MIB agents J and K (Smith and Jones) avert catastrophe at the last moment. A third sequel is apparently in pre-production.

Chapter 6 – The influence on current technology

Science-fiction authors describe many weird and wonderful technologies in their works, but how many of these futuristic gadgets are in development and has their writing influenced what we already use today?

Antigravity devices have been in the pipeline for as long as the force has been understood. However, despite claims by Russian scientist Dr Yevgeny Podkletnov that he has developed a machine for altering gravity, nothing so far produced has worked. The problem seems to revolve around the

The Large Hadron Collider at CERN.

mechanisms by which gravity works. Essentially, gravity is a product of the warping of spacetime by any object with mass. We all bend space and time but, as we have such little mass, we don't really notice it.

Planets, stars and galaxies, of course, are considerably more massive. Overcoming their gravity, which is the key to cheap spaceflight and travel between solar systems, must have been mastered by any UFOs visiting us. The problem is that we don't *fully* understand how gravity works. Current scientific thinking suggests that a minute particle in the centre of atoms, the as yet undiscovered graviton, is what mediates the force of gravity. If we find this particle (the Large Hadron Collider at CERN – the European centre for nuclear research in Switzerland – might locate it during one of its millions of experimental collisions), we might eventually be able to manipulate it, and that could result in the production of antigravity devices.

Time travel might also be possible if we can manipulate

gravity, because it will give us some control over the fabric of spacetime. By effectively folding space back on itself, we could travel to distant parts of the cosmos in a fraction of the time it would take in a conventional spacecraft, faster even than the time it would take light to make the journey.

Even if spacetime can't be manipulated, the faster a spaceship travels, the quicker it moves into the future. So, if UFOs have ever visited us, travelling billions of miles across space at incredible speeds, they could arrive back at their home planet thousands of years in the future. To do this would require propulsion systems that have not yet been invented on Earth. Perhaps one day the aliens will share the blueprints for their antimatter reactors, hypersonic combustion ramjets, wormhole generators, magnetoplasma rockets, ion drives, teleportation devices and antigravity systems with us, or maybe they already have…

It has long been suggested that the American Telephone and Telegraph (AT&T) Company has only made scientific and technological breakthroughs because it had access to the alien spacecraft that crashed at Roswell and has undertaken a huge reverse engineering project. Together with Bell Laboratories, the two giants ran the US nuclear arsenal for nearly half a century.

In 1949 President Truman approved a contract for AT&T to derive as much technology from the nuclear bomb project as it could. This resulted in a top-secret Z-Division being created, its aim being to use the physics to design new weapons, electronics, guidance systems, transistors, lasers and integrated circuits. Some believe, however, that rapid advances in technology in the 1940s and 1950s can only have been made if alien equipment had been reverse engineered. It has even been rumoured that the US launched a nuclear missile platform into space called Sky Station using a craft based on the Roswell UFO.

Aliens piloting UFOs to our solar system are bound to have developed advanced medicinal techniques to help them survive the long interplanetary journey and recover from illnesses or injuries sustained along the way. We will have much to learn from their methods and treatments. Minute nanotechnological robots will be used to repair damaged tissues and replicator cells (like our stem cells) will be used to replace worn out limbs and organs. In the quest for immortality, we are already trying to understand the processes by which these treatments work.

Chapter 7 – Museums, exhibitions and websites for UFO fans

If you are a fan of science, the universe and UFOs, then the Exhibition of the Universe (formerly the Alien & UFO exhibition) in the Golden Mile Centre on the central promenade in Blackpool is worth a visit. This tourist attraction was built by spiritualist and supernaturalist David Boyle. The *Dr Who* exhibition and museum boasting many of the original props and costumes from the science-fiction TV series can also be found in the town centre.

The International UFO Museum and Research Centre in Roswell has a vast stockpile of information about the apparent crash of an alien spacecraft in New Mexico in 1947. It has collected and preserved both material and information in several forms of media (written, audio and visual) relating to the event, as well as housing a number of exhibits devoted to unexplained UFO phenomena from across the globe. The museum is highly regarded as a leading source of scientific, anecdotal and up-to-date information on UFO events. Admission costs from $2 - $5.

The museum hosts an annual UFO festival, with the 2012 event running from July 1-3, when sceptics and believers will come together to celebrate one of the most debated incidents in UFO history. There will be guest speakers, sci-fi and science authors, live entertainment, costume contests and many family-friendly activities.

The museum can be found at:

114 North Main
Roswell
NM 88201
USA
Tel: 505-625-949
www.roswellufomuseum.com

Founded by the Sirius UFO Space Science Research Centre and sponsored by Funika, the International UFO Museum in the historic city of Istanbul in Turkey opened in 2002. It is the only major museum dedicated to the UFO phenomenon in all of Central and Eastern Europe, the Balkans and the Middle East. The museum is divided into three sections: the museum and exhibition centre consists of photographs, illustrations, models and documents in Turkish and English; the library chronicles sightings worldwide, boasts information about archaeological remains and the view of ancient cultures on aliens, and keeps documents about crop circles, Area 51 and other bases, alien abductions, declassified official documents, NASA cover-ups, university research and analysis relating to Mars, and hundreds of newspaper and magazine articles; and there is also a video conference suite.

The UFO Museum in Hakui City, Japan, opened in July 1996. Although it's primarily a museum devoted to space science and exploration, it has several UFO-related artefacts, including recently declassified documents. There are also displays and studies into unidentified aerial phenomena, alien abductions, crop circles, UFO contacts, and SETI radio transmissions.

Opened in 2004, the Seattle Museum of Mysteries is run by The Seattle UFO and Paranormal Group. This historic museum is open to all ages and has permanent exhibitions, stunning pictures and documents relating to the Maury Island UFO sighting in 1947, which includes previously classified FBI papers. It also documents the Kenneth Arnold sighting of nine discs near Mt. Rainier, which led to the phrase flying saucer entering our language. There is also a feature on crop circles in Washington State and an extensive library. Lecturers on the paranormal, ancient civilizations, UFOs and other mysteries speak at an annual event each June.

The ten most popular fan sites are listed overleaf:

www.alien-ufos.com
www.ufoinfo.com
www.abovetopsecret.com
www.latest-ufo-sightings.net
www.ufoevidence.org
www.ufo-blogger.com
www.theufosecret.com
www.aliensonearth.com/area51
www.dreamlandresort.com
www.roswellfiles.com

Gerald Haines, historian at the National Reconnaissance Office who studied secret files on UFOs for the CIA, believes that over half of all the UFO reports in the 1950s and 1960s were accounted for by manned reconnaissance flights.

Indeed, it seems likely that the lights seen by the crew of America West 564 in May 1995 were probably that of a secret military aircraft – North American Air Defence (NORAD) radar picked up the object but then denied anything else had been in the air – likewise the similar sighting reported by the crew of a cargo aircraft above New Zealand in 1978, and unusual lights seen by both Ray Bowyer (over the Channel Islands in 2007) and Captain Jean-Charles Duboc (Paris, 1994) can possibly be explained as either sun dogs (ice halos reflecting sunlight) or mirror-like illusions created by warm air inversion, but some UFO sightings will always remain inexplicable...